I Hate My Brother Harry

MEAN HARRY

written by Crescent Dragonwagon

illustrated by Dick Gackenbach

Harper & Row, Publishers

Library of Congress Cataloging in Publication Data
Dragonwagon, Crescent. 1952–
   I hate my brother Harry.

   Summary: Nobody believes Harry's little sister
hates him, and even she is confused by the way he
treats her.
   [1. Brothers and sisters–Fiction]   I. Gackenbach,
Dick, ill.   II. Title.
PZ7.D7824Iab 1983   [E]   82-47706
ISBN 0-06-021757-X
ISBN 0-06-021758-8 (lib. bdg.)

For Stephen, who once,

for his sister,

drew eyes on a pig.

I hate my brother Harry.

When my Aunt Jane asks me on the phone, "How is Harry?" I say, "He is fine, but I hate him."

She doesn't believe me.

She says, "Oh, you don't hate your brother."

But I do.

No one believes I hate my brother.

Harry is seven years older than me.

He is mean.

He is too old to play with his electric trains, but he won't let *me* play with them.

He says, "They were mine, and they *are* mine. I don't want a stupid little sister like you ruining *my* trains.

"No, it isn't very nice of Harry," says my father, "but they *are* his trains."

I hate Harry.

"No, you don't," says my father.

But I do.

Once, when I was in the bathroom upstairs, I left the door open. Nobody was home but my mother. Then Harry came home with two of his friends. They ran upstairs.

When Harry saw me he started screaming.

"Can't you even close the door? Don't you know anything? You are so stupid, stupid, stupid! I don't believe how stupid you are!"

He grabbed the bathroom door, and he slammed it, hard.

My mother said, "You aren't stupid, honey. He was just embarrassed because his friends were with him."

But I hate Harry.

I wish he would meet someone bigger and meaner than he is.

I wish they would say to him, "I'll get you, Harry," and yell, "Stupid, stupid, stupid."

Sometimes Harry pretends to be nice.

"Would you like to bake some brownies?" he says.

He lets me open the box and pour in the water.

He holds the heavy glass bowl and lets me stir with a wooden spoon. Then he opens the can of walnuts and pours them in, and I stir some more.

We scrape the sticky brown batter into a pan and put it in the oven to bake.

Sometimes he even lets me lick the bowl.

But then he kicks me out.

He won't let me in till he's frosted the brownies.

The frosting he makes is this awful green and brown color.

"It has chopped-up frogs in it," he tells me.

So I don't eat the brownies.

"All the more for me," Harry says. "Mmmm. I *love* that Frog Frosting."

"Harry, don't upset your sister," says my father.

To me, he says, "Honey, he's only kidding. You can eat your brownies. They don't have frogs in them."

But when my father isn't looking, Harry says–just with his mouth–"Yes, they *do.*"

So I don't eat them.

I hate Harry.

"Oh no, you don't," says my father. "You *dislike* Harry sometimes, but you don't hate him."

I do.

I wish a giant frog would catch him and make him into frosting.

When I was little, Harry told me, "You know about the snakes, don't you? The big snakes that hide in beds? They come out in the dark, and as soon as the blankets get wrinkled up, they wrap around your neck."

For a long time I slept on my pillow, so I wouldn't wrinkle the blankets.

Finally I asked my mother about the snakes.

"Snakes in blankets?" she said. "Of course not, honey! Where on earth did you get that idea?"

"Harry told me," I said.

"You shouldn't believe everything Harry says," she said. "He likes to tease you."

But it wasn't teasing.

It was mean.

I hate Harry.

I hope a snake wraps around his neck.

Whenever we have chocolate pudding, Harry whispers to me, "I spit in the pudding."

My father asks me, "Why aren't you eating your pudding?"

"Because Harry spit in it," I say.

"No, he didn't," says my father, "did you, Harry?"

"No," says Harry. "Yuck. She's so gross. She always has such gross ideas."

"Harry, do not call your sister gross," says my father. "Honey, eat your pudding."

I hate Harry.

Someday I will spit in his pudding and I won't tell him I did it, either.

I wish Harry was like the nice brothers on TV and in books.

I know he could be. Sometimes he is.

When I had chicken pox, Harry walked all the way to the library to get books for me. Then he read them to me out loud.

And sometimes when he has to baby-sit for me, he gives me fun baths. He lets me put in as much bubblebath as I want, and we make seal noises and pretend to be seals.

He washes my back and draws letters of the alphabet on it with water. "Guess what letter it is."

"Is it a B?" I say.

"No," he says, "but you were close. It's an R. B is just like an R, but closed on the bottom."

Sometimes he lets me draw pictures in *his* room.

Once he let me use his new Magic Markers.

Why can't he always be like that?

Once he let me stay in the kitchen and make Frog Frosting with him.

"It's just vanilla frosting," he said. "But then you do this." And he put three drops of every kind of food coloring in, and said, "Now stir and see what happens."

I stirred and stirred.

First that white frosting had trails of bright blue and yellow and red and green in it. Then the colors all ran together and turned the frosting a greenish-brown frog color.

"Taste it," said Harry.

I did. It still tasted like vanilla.

"Why do you make it that color, Harry?" I asked.

"Because then nobody else wants to eat it," he said. But then he said, "I really do put frogs in it most of the time, though. I just did it with food coloring once to fool you."

I hate him.

"If you really hated him," says my mother, "you couldn't like him sometimes."

But I do.

I like him sometimes, but mostly I hate him.

My mother says, "When you were very little, Harry was nice to you a lot."

"Name one time," I say.

"I can name lots of times," says my mother. "When I first brought you home from the hospital, Harry would stand by the crib for hours, just watching you."

"Just because he watched me doesn't mean he liked me," I say.

"True," says my mother. "But sometimes he'd also put his hand in the crib and let you wrap your tiny fingers around his big index finger. And he would show you off to his friends. "Look at my baby sister!" he'd say. And once you wiggled around in the crib so that your head was under the blankets. Harry ran to get me. He was scared you might smother."

"What else did he do?" I say.

"One winter night when you were almost two, you couldn't sleep. Harry said, 'I know! Let's take her for a walk! She'll like it.' So we bundled you up in your snowsuit and boots and a silly little knitted hat with a tassel and ear flaps. And we stuffed you in your stroller. You were so bundled up you hardly fit. Harry pushed you all the way to Sedalia Park and back."

"Did I like it?" I asked her. "Did Harry like it?"

"You loved it," says my mother. "It was the first time you had been out at night. Harry showed you everything. 'See the stars?' he'd say. 'See the trees? See the park?' I remember he said to me, 'She looks like an owl, and she loves the night like an owl.' And you did. With your eyes wide open and all those clothes on, you looked like an owl with its feathers puffed up. And the next morning at breakfast, Harry said to you, 'How are you, Owl?'"

"If Harry liked me then, why does he hate me now?" I ask my mother.

"It's something brothers and sisters go through," says my mother. "Your Aunt Jane and I used to fight. But it's not hating. You'll see. When you grow up you'll probably be friends."

One day I decided to give Harry a secret test.

I wrote him a letter and left it on his desk. The letter had a picture of a pig. The pig had sharp ears and a curly tail, but no eyes.

My letter said:

> *Dear Harry,*
> *If you would like to be friends,*
> *please put eyes on this pig.*

The next day when I woke up, the pig was on my dresser. Harry had drawn eyes on it and also he made it smoking a cigar. I was glad he did that.

But he never said anything about the letter, and he is still mean.

I still hate him most of the time.

I really do.

But then I think, well…
he did draw eyes on that pig.